I0664527

Family - An Odyssey

Valerie J Runyan

Published by Desert Lighthouse Publishing, 2026.

FAMILY-AN ODYSEY
First edition January 1, 2026
Copyright © 2026 Valerie J Runyan
ISBN: 979-8218872038
Library of Congress Control Number: 2025925838
Written by Valerie J Runyan

Table of Contents

FAMILY- AN ODYSSEY VALERIE J RUNYAN

FAMILY- AN ODYSSEY VALERIE J RUNYAN

FAMILY- AN ODYSSEY VALERIE J RUNYAN

FAMILY- AN ODYSSEY VALERIE J RUNYAN

FAMILY- AN ODYSSEY VALERIE J RUNYAN

FAMILY- AN ODYSSEY VALERIE J RUNYAN

FAMILY- AN ODYSSEY VALERIE J RUNYAN

FAMILY- AN ODYSSEY VALERIE J RUNYAN

FAMILY- AN ODYSSEY VALERIE J RUNYAN

FAMILY- AN ODYSSEY VALERIE J RUNYAN

FAMILY- AN ODYSSEY VALERIE J RUNYAN

FAMILY- AN ODYSSEY VALERIE J RUNYAN

FAMILY- AN ODYSSEY VALERIE J RUNYAN

FAMILY-AN ODYSSEY VALERIE J RUNYAN

FAMILY- AN ODYSSEY VALERIE J RUNYAN

FAMILY- AN ODYSSEY VALERIE J RUNYAN

FAMILY- AN ODYSSEY VALERIE J RUNYAN

FAMILY- AN ODYSSEY VALERIE J RUNYAN

FAMILY- AN ODYSSEY VALERIE J RUNYAN

FAMILY- AN ODYSSEY VALERIE J RUNYAN

FAMILY- AN ODYSSEY VALERIE J RUNYAN

FAMILY- AN ODYSSEY VALERIE J RUNYAN

FAMILY- AN ODYSSEY VALERIE J RUNYAN

FAMILY- AN ODYSSEY VALERIE J RUNYAN
FAMILY- AN ODYSSEY VALERIE J RUNYAN
FAMILY-AN ODYSSEY VALERIE J RUNYAN

DEDICATION

THE HUMAN FAMILY IS A NEVER-ENDING ODYSSEY OF-
ORIGINAL CREATED CHOSEN

FAMILY- AN ODYSSEY VALERIE J RUNYAN
FAMILY- AN ODYSSEY VALERIE J RUNYAN
FAMILY- AN ODYSSEY VALERIE J RUNYAN
FAMILY- AN ODYSSEY VALERIE J RUNYAN
FAMILY- AN ODYSSEY VALERIE J RUNYAN
FAMILY- AN ODYSSEY VALERIE J RUNYAN
FAMILY- AN ODYSSEY VALERIE J RUNYAN
FAMILY- AN ODYSSEY VALERIE J RUNYAN
FAMILY- AN ODYSSEY VALERIE J RUNYAN
FAMILY- AN ODYSSEY VALERIE J RUNYAN
FAMILY- AN ODYSSEY VALERIE J RUNYAN
FAMILY- AN ODYSSEY VALERIE J RUNYAN
FAMILY-AN ODYSSEY VALERIE J RUNYAN
FAMILY- AN ODYSSEY VALERIE J RUNYAN
FAMILY- AN ODYSSEY VALERIE J RUNYAN
FAMILY- AN ODYSSEY VALERIE J RUNYAN
FAMILY- AN ODYSSEY VALERIE J RUNYAN
FAMILY- AN ODYSSEY VALERIE J RUNYAN
FAMILY- AN ODYSSEY VALERIE J RUNYAN
FAMILY- AN ODYSSEY VALERIE J RUNYAN
FAMILY- AN ODYSSEY VALERIE J RUNYAN
FAMILY- AN ODYSSEY VALERIE J RUNYAN

CHAPTER I. SATURDAYS

I've loved Saturdays since I was about five or six years old, I clearly remember cartoons going from black and white to technicolor.

The word "Technicolor" seemed so fancy to my young mind, my mother laughed every time I said it properly, she said that it was a sign that I was becoming a bright sophisticated young man.

Her praise pleased me, and all I ever wanted to do every chance I got, was to be the center of her praise.

Growing up in the seventies in the *San Fernando Valley,* which are the suburbs of *Los Angeles, California* she and I became each other's better halves.

When I was too hyper for her depressed mood we would lay in her huge to me bed, crafted of dark heavily hand-carved wood with flowers on the head and footboards, spirals on the four tall posts that she draped with sheer pastel scarves, creating two almost see through walls.

In her bed that she did not share with my father, we would leisurely leaf through issues of *Vogue* magazine where I learned fashion designer's names and styles, by the time I was twelve.

In an effort to help her feel better, I would play Frank Sinatra vinyl albums on her vintage record player that had a clear plastic top cover, which sat atop the gold veined marble vanity table the dark wood and fabric covered speakers, were tucked against the far wall on either side of the four drawer bureau that matched her bed.

The matching wardrobe and accompanying squared three-sided lighted vanity mirror, plus the settee with the same elegantly carved legs, along with the plush dark magenta cushion all of this made her bedroom a sanctuary.

In my adolescent years on Saturdays, I got to leave the house in the morning and didn't have to return until sunset with my *Los Angeles Unified School District* student ID, I covered the "City of Angels" like I was running for mayor every weekend, the *Garment District* was my "City Hall" and every little thrift store was my constituent.

When my mother was up to accompanying me, it was like we were the newly-elected Governor and First Lady of California, and it was our Inauguration Day with *Rodeo Drive* being our parade route where we perfected our "royalty wave."

All doors parted for us and money was no object, food was served on the best China and flatware along with the finest linen, our crystal glasses never empty.

Through those years, we filled her wardrobe with vintage designer labels from merchants who simply didn't know, or care about the treasures we walked out the door with.

In my mid-teens those glorious Saturdays became fewer and farther between, then came the one when she asked me to start spending some of my beloved Saturdays inside the house with my father, I acquiesced and she praised me but I somehow knew that would be the last time, I would be the center of her praise.

I got to miss a whole week of school, I had to find a dictionary to look up the word "Bereavement" because I over-heard one of the teachers whispering a little too loudly, that I was apparently experiencing it.

For my *SAT Prep Tutorials* I wrote several essays about my mother's suicide, which my English Literature teacher sent off to some literary publication and as a third-place prize they sent me my very own dictionary, along with a letter of high praise that I would continue my blossoming writing career, and they hoped to read more from me in the future.

I wrote them a return letter, thanking them for their kind words but they would not be reading anything from me again because, I planned to design furniture.

I began to enjoy being with my father because he was actually present and not out golfing and playing tennis, or wining and dining new clients for the law firm he worked at my whole life he had made Senior Managing Partner long ago, probably when he had moved into his study so as not to disturb my mother when he worked or just came home too late.

We would go grocery shopping for the week, at either *Trader Joe's* or *Whole Food's* depending on when we woke up from a Friday night movie marathon on *Turner Classic Movies*, watching on of our favorite black and white female movie stars.

In my late-teens my Saturdays changed yet again, when my father began to unceremoniously drop me off at nine a.m. sharp at one of my aunt's and their loud husband's homes, I found solace and solitude in the women's closets to sketch my wardrobes bureaus and dressers.

Almost all my aunts whispered loudly to one another about something being wrong with me, on the other hand their husbands shouted that there was nothing wrong with me, because I liked to watch *Bob Villa's Home Improvement* shows with them.

I broached the subject of our family tree with my father three Saturdays in a row, because he purposely evaded my questions I became disinterested in him, or in doing anything else with him from then on.

One Saturday the one aunt who didn't partake in the gossip about my situation, took me into her upstairs walk-in closet full of vintage designer clothes that I ran my fingertips through feel of

Chiffon, Taffeta, wool Jersey, Silk, Crepe de chine and *Cotton Knit* were so familiar to me because they had belonged to my mother.

Her walk-in included her vanity table with its three-sided soft pink lightbulb framed makeup mirror, the expensive marble with the light gold veins running through it made it look so elegant, the plush velour settee was the same color as my mother's, and all of her designer shoes had three-inch heels.

The Saturday before my high-school graduation, this particular aunt to me to what she called a "Buyer's Warehouse" for wardrobe industry professionals, the people who dress actors and actresses for television shows and motion pictures.

In that warehouse I felt at home settled and finally at peace, it must have showed because she said the most wonderful words I had heard so far in my young life, "Do you want to try something on?"

She led me to a small dressing room with a long white fake marble makeup counter, with a fingerprint smudged lengthwise mirror accompanied by four large round soft pink lightbulbs above it.

As I undressed, I felt as if I were shedding uncomfortable clothes that didn't quite fit me, but now I was about to slip into fabric that embraced my body naturally.

Back out into the showroom I stood in front of a full-length mirror, in my first *Coco Chanel* skirt suit it was the iconic Ivory White/Black Ink Houndstooth pattern, in a size two.

The three-quarter length sleeves fell precisely just past my elbows, the jacket settled nicely at the top of my hips, the skirt hem stopped tastefully below my kneecaps.

I surprised myself at how easily I took my very first steps in a pair of three-inch ivory designer sling-backs, with the ivory clutch and black elbow length gloves, I felt like *Jackie-O* herself.

I recall being startled by my aunt's voice because I thought I was dreaming, I think she said something to the effect of "You look beautiful." I couldn't take my eyes off my reflection.

I started laughing then crying, I wondered how the human mind can comprehend joy and pain in the same instant, how the human heart can accept both in the same moment, the human body can only collapse.

I still think about my favorite aunt sometimes, because if it weren't for her and her husband taking me in, when my own father rejected me at my mother's funeral just because I wore her vintage *Halston*.

I will be eternally grateful to her for taking me to *The Center* Downtown, where I met "the girls" we bonded over our obsessive love for *Diane von Frustenberg* wrap dresses, that day became our "Gotcha Day" right then and there we decided to become our own little family.

They cheered the loudest when I delivered my high school commencement speech wearing a *Bob Mackie* gown, then on my eighteenth birthday we drove to Las Vegas in my brand-new car, most likely courtesy from him.

We weathered the long-distance relationship thing when two of us went to *University Nevada Las Vegas*, and the other two went to *The Fashion Institute* we reunited for good with degrees and job prospects in Las Vegas, where we vowed to never live more than ten minutes away from each other.

They followed their passion for fashion and costume design, while I love furniture and interior designing for one of the very few one-stop shop, planned neighborhood architecture firms in the country.

My heart and soul will always belong to fashion, I indulge this side of myself every other Sunday afternoon with brunch with "the girls" I also get dressed in vintage designer gowns every other Saturday night, for cocktails cigarettes and jazz at my favorite local lounge.

FAMILY- AN ODYSSEY VALERIE J RUNYAN

FAMILY- AN ODYSSEY VALERIE J RUNYAN

FAMILY- AN ODYSSEY VALERIE J RUNYAN

FAMILY- AN ODYSSEY VALERIE J RUNYAN

FAMILY- AN ODYSSEY VALERIE J RUNYAN

FAMILY- AN ODYSSEY VALERIE J RUNYAN

FAMILY- AN ODYSSEY VALERIE J RUNYAN

FAMILY- AN ODYSSEY VALERIE J RUNYAN

FAMILY- AN ODYSSEY VALERIE J RUNYAN

FAMILY- AN ODYSSEY VALERIE J RUNYAN

FAMILY- AN ODYSSEY VALERIE J RUNYAN

FAMILY- AN ODYSSEY VALERIE J RUNYAN

FAMILY-AN ODYSSEY VALERIE J RUNYAN

FAMILY- AN ODYSSEY VALERIE J RUNYAN

FAMILY- AN ODYSSEY VALERIE J RUNYAN

FAMILY- AN ODYSSEY VALERIE J RUNYAN

FAMILY- AN ODYSSEY VALERIE J RUNYAN

FAMILY- AN ODYSSEY VALERIE J RUNYAN

FAMILY- AN ODYSSEY VALERIE J RUNYAN

FAMILY- AN ODYSSEY VALERIE J RUNYAN

FAMILY- AN ODYSSEY VALERIE J RUNYAN

FAMILY- AN ODYSSEY VALERIE J RUNYAN

CHAPTER II. DRESSED

I love waking up early, with the sun painting golden rays on my walls through my vintage lace bedroom curtains, I hate to leave my new *Ralph Lauren "Allaire"* bed with the luscious smell of *Elizabeth Taylor's White Diamonds* Silk Spun Body Powder all over my sheets.

I have inquiring neighbors- this is Las Vegas after all, so I shouldn't perform my morning salutations and Tai Chi in my short dragon embroidered silk kimono the ex-girlfriend, who left me for authentic Sushi and a fashion designer, sent me from Japan as a housewarming present.

Yesterday's hot yoga was a little too hot, so Rainier bumped some of his least favorite clients just for me today why not take advantage of his little crush on me, speaking of crushes that gorgeous beauty school apprentice at the *Lotus Salon and Day Spa*, she's the only woman I trust with a straight razor near this face.

I wouldn't mind at all, if I happen to die by drowning in those lovely brown eyes, her dimples are just the cutest, her touch electrifies my skin, and she always smells like a bouquet of red roses.

I hope she'll be pleased when I stroll in wearing my favorite red, white and black *Sean John* tracksuit, with the first pair of *Air Jordan's* I ever bought in the same color scheme, for my by-monthly indulgence.

Sometimes having my hands moisturized, nails buffed and trimmed by her is quite arousing, so I have to concentrate a little harder on which shade of blush tint I want to be complimented on, by my coworkers.

Damn I love my rain shower I almost hate to get out, but today is not the day to show up fashionably late for brunch with the "girls", I live for Saturday brunch and the weekly gossip-go-round, since we've been our own chosen family for a decade and a half now.

I love my "girls" so much, not only for their bravery and boldness to live their true lives out loud every day, they are the queens of my life but I'm just not there yet.

I can only live my inside outside every other Saturday night, but right now for brunch at the *Lotus Flower Café and Bakery*, I'm feeling my Armani suite with various shades of grey accessories and, my brand new heather grey Louboutin suede loafers sans socks.

I can't wait to see who else will be on display, we've all been vintage designer clothes horses since, we all went crazy over the same *Diane von Frustenberg* black and white wrap dress.

When we all get together we are literally and figuratively the rainbow flag, and we dress to impress mostly each other *Chanel*, *Dior*, and *Mackie* came out to play, even *Lacroix* made an appearance, we absolutely love the jaw dropping attention we get.

The three of them have jobs where they can be themselves, sure I'm lead designer at a socially conscious architecture firm that plans diverse neighborhoods, but they're just not that woke yet I can't wear a *Givenchy* suit in the morning meeting, and then *Vivian Westwood* frock in the afternoon for a client consultation.

On the way back from brunch, a white Corvette containing a tiny woman passed me up blasting Shania Twain's *Man, I Feel Like A Woman*, I was singing it in the shower.

If imitation is the sincerest form of flattery, then my favorite aunt would be extremely flattered, I've built the vanity room of my dreams, very much like the one she had.

I just couldn't do the Ecru white carpet plus she didn't have a window, I love these Heather gray and Lavender floral wall tapestries and matching carpet, it's really quite soothing.

You simply can't beat a Granite countertop for beauty and value, the back-lit three panel make-up mirrors are also a great addition, although a chandelier would be the best investment when I make Mariah Carey money someday.

Tonight, I finally get to wear the repaired *Alexander McQueen* gown "the girls" bought last month at a charity silent auction in L.A. along with my new *Manolo Blahnik* black suede stilettos, a borrowed but never returned *Kate Spade* clutch, and to complete this perfect ensemble the new Lauren Bacall "S" wave on the right side wig, just like in her publicity photos.

I love the smell of sandalwood incense, which blends perfectly with this special playlist I created especially for these Saturday nights, when I get dressed, I realized a while ago that it has a lot of Frank Sinatra especially his *Capitol Years*.

Frank sings *Strangers In The Night* as I debate between size 32B and 34B gel boobs, while smoothing on *White Diamonds* body lotion Frank and I duet *Fly Me To The Moon*.

This new Victoria Secret V-Wire Black Mesh and Lace Teddy fits real nice not too snug, and *Berkshire's Shimmers* black lace top stockings never disappoint, *Max Factor* is the only make-up I will ever put on this face, it was good enough for Katherine Hepburn, Marlene Deitrich and of course Lauren Bacall.

My father and I started watching their films while my mother slept, which was a lot because of her severe depression, but that ended and it eventually broke us when she committed suicide.

I wore her vintage *Halston* to her funeral, that was the last time he and I had any personal contact, the last thing he said to my face, was that he could not and would not accept a cross dressing son, so I moved in with my favorite aunt who had that amazing vanity room.

The *Fireside Lounge* is this little gem on the Las Vegas "Strip" has such a beautiful atmosphere, with thick red crushed velvet dining chairs, that goes so perfectly with the heavy Oak claw foot dining tables.

The heavy velvet ornate draped curtains dividing the dining room from the stage, it's large enough to fit the Jazz Quartet band, and their sultry soul singer who perform every other Saturday night.

The acoustics are amazing in this space, with the completely awesome centerpiece gas fireplace, soft plush red velvet settees encircle it, light teakwood bench tables with square cork coasters completes this elegant atmosphere.

I like to sit at the bar with the high back chairs that match the plush settees, the bar itself is a dark coffee stain, with soft pink overhead lighting bouncing off the beveled glass behind the bar look like tiny rainbows, plus the premium alcohols is the best.

I usually have an *Absolute* Martini with one Greek olive, but tonight I'm feeling like a *Tanqueray* Martini with a Spanish olive, I limit myself to smoking my *Delicados Cigarros Filtros 24* to these Saturday nights when I get dressed, I like the fact that I know everyone who frequents this World Famous Las Vegas landmark.

From Charles the weekend bartender, who has been shopping his same *Romantic Dramady* screenplay for the last five years, to the once a month San Diego State *Contemporary Music Theory* professor who drives up here in his sister's minivan, where he sometimes gets laid.

But tonight a new man has arrived and sits down next to me, his cologne smells so familiar as I put the cigarette to my matte rouge lips I turn toward him, I can't believe he is being quite the gentleman offering me a light and another drink, but what this man doesn't even know is that the "woman" he has just bought another drink for, is his own son.

I rarely miss yoga I just can't think about anything else, but this fucking card that asshole left next to my glass last night, "the girls" did such a fantastic job on that *Alexander McQueen* gown I'd been dying to wear and I was having a perfectly good time, until he showed up with all his baggage and painful memories.

I was not and still am not prepared for this flood of memories, but I'm not going to fail my therapy, so today belongs to remembering, feeling and letting go... again.

FAMILY- AN ODYSSEY VALERIE J RUNYAN
FAMILY- AN ODYSSEY VALERIE J RUNYAN
FAMILY- AN ODYSSEY VALERIE J RUNYAN
FAMILY- AN ODYSSEY VALERIE J RUNYAN
FAMILY- AN ODYSSEY VALERIE J RUNYAN
FAMILY- AN ODYSSEY VALERIE J RUNYAN
FAMILY- AN ODYSSEY VALERIE J RUNYAN
FAMILY- AN ODYSSEY VALERIE J RUNYAN
FAMILY- AN ODYSSEY VALERIE J RUNYAN
FAMILY- AN ODYSSEY VALERIE J RUNYAN
FAMILY- AN ODYSSEY VALERIE J RUNYAN
FAMILY- AN ODYSSEY VALERIE J RUNYAN
FAMILY- AN ODYSSEY VALERIE J RUNYAN
FAMILY-AN ODYSSEY VALERIE J RUNYAN
FAMILY- AN ODYSSEY VALERIE J RUNYAN
FAMILY- AN ODYSSEY VALERIE J RUNYAN
FAMILY- AN ODYSSEY VALERIE J RUNYAN
FAMILY- AN ODYSSEY VALERIE J RUNYAN
FAMILY- AN ODYSSEY VALERIE J RUNYAN
FAMILY- AN ODYSSEY VALERIE J RUNYAN
FAMILY- AN ODYSSEY VALERIE J RUNYAN
FAMILY- AN ODYSSEY VALERIE J RUNYAN

FAMILY- AN ODYSSEY VALERIE J RUNYAN

FAMILY- AN ODYSSEY VALERIE J RUNYAN

FAMILY-AN ODYSSEY VALERIE J RUNYAN

CHAPTER III. TIME

FATHER
"Nice loafers."

PARALEGAL
"Thanks *Louboutin's*, my girlfriend got them for me, first day and all at a new firm."

FATHER
"Yeah I recognize the expensive red soles, guess that's why you're one of my bosses."

PARALEGAL
"Wait, what?"

FATHER
"And your secret's safe with me, I fucking hate therapy too especially for my marriage."

PARALEGAL
"I wasn't there for marriage counseling, I was there for anger management and if you say one homophobic thing to me, I will put you in the ground, are we clear?"

FATHER
"Absolutely, I have no intentions of pissing off my boss my first day here."

PARALEGAL
"Day's not over yet and stop calling me your boss, you're my boss I'm your paralegal, which means for you I don't work past five-thirty weekdays, and I do not work any weekend because unlike you lawyers I have a life outside this office."

FATHER
"As your boss I completely accept that, I hope this is the start of a good working relationship, welcome aboard."

PARALEGAL
"Thanks sorry about the hostility, I'm working on that."

FATHER
"I'd say you're making progress, but I have no comparison, yet."

PARALEGAL
"I smacked my former boss with his own briefcase, for saying I'm a tree he'd

like to climb."

FATHER

"Oh."

PARALEGAL

"That was the last straw, other straws were 'you're too pretty to be a lesbian' and 'you're not gay, you just haven't met the right dick yet' or the one, when my girlfriend came to the office, for my birthday lunch I heard 'I'd like to be the meat in that sandwich' they are so very fortunate, I didn't burn that tinderbox down to the ground when I left the next day."

FATHER

"I see, well I certainly would prefer you as an ally rather than an adversary, friends?"

PARALEGAL

"Sure, at least in this building."

PARAFATHER

"Great, now let's go see our office."

PARALEGAL

"Holy shit, look at this ocean view!"

FATHER

"Yeah, you should see the other side at night, the lights are spectacular."

PARALEGAL

"Well thank God for Daylight Savings Time, guess I'll see it then."

FATHER

"Come on, we don't want to be late for our first morning briefing."

PARALEGAL

"How do you know your way around here already?"

FATHER

"I was here Saturday and Sunday, just to get the lay of the land."

PARALEGAL

"Typical lawyer you know your family life is going to suffer right? And before you row down that river of denial, trust me it will, my dad was one my whole life until he died behind his desk and was found by the cleaning lady, not a great legacy to leave behind, just sayin."

FATHER

(MONOLOGUE)

The short flight from *Harry Reid International* in Las Vegas back to *LAX-Los Angeles International,* was just enough time for me to write my retirement memo and have two *Jack and Cokes,* when you know for sure how much time you have left, you start thinking about the places where you don't want to die, my seven month final countdown started three weeks ago honestly I thought my liver would give out before my lungs, but it's a crap shoot when you spend your entire adult life smoking and drinking.

PARALEGAL

"They still have the best steaks, even after all these years!"

FATHER

"It was stipulated in the owner's will I executed, that his kids not change one damn thing in this restaurant, or he would haunt them for the rest of their lives, hauntings aren't legally binding but they must have believed him."

PARALEGAL

"Either that, or they believe that you will buy them out with your fifty-one percent stock share, leaving them penniless and being Millennials, they'll simply walk away and go be vegan or gluten-free or NON-GMO, or some shit somewhere else."

FATHER

"And leave the big bad city to us old folks, here's to Los Angeles, home sweet home!"

PARALEGAL

"I'll drink to that, until Monday at least."

FATHER

"You sent my retirement email?"

PARALEGAL

"Yep and mine, everyone will see them come Monday I still can't believe we did it, after how many years?"

FATHER

"Too many our whole adult lives, hey remember our first day when I thought you were my boss?"

PARALEGAL

"Wait a minute before we start down memory lane, did you go, did you see...

FATHER

"Yeah, I saw him."

PARALEGAL

"And?"

FATHER

"And I got freaked out again, but not like before I bought him another Martini, and lit his cigarette, but I left him my card."

PARALEGAL

"You left your own son, your old law firm's business card!"

FATHER

"I panicked, just like I did when I saw him in his mother's suit at her funeral, the same one she wore on our wedding day, yeah I know I'm a fucking shitty father... still."

PARALEGAL

"No you're not, you've changed you've grown you've even become a little woke-ish, and that's something."

FATHER

"Obviously not, I still can't see him like that, in that way."

PARALEGAL

"Maybe not yet but you will, you have to, before it's too late before you..."

FATHER

"Don't say it I know I'm dying, you don't have to remind me."

PARALEGAL

"Yes. I. Fucking. Do! Because your ass will wallow around in this sad little pity mud hole, wasting this precious time you have left to re-connect with your one and only son, who is a mere four and a half hour drive away in Las Vegas, so shit yeah I have to remind you that you're dying!"

FATHER

"Well as long as we're doing all this reminding, let me remind you that if I hadn't accidently elbowed you in your boobs during that basketball game, you wouldn't have gone to the doctor who asked when was your last mammogram, which led to them finding breast cancer!"

PARALEGAL

"Yeah well thanks for that painful body check, the double mastectomy was no picnic thanks for covering for me, all those mornings."

FATHER

"Well thanks for covering for me, when I came in hung over especially after lunch."

PARALEGAL

"That's what friends are for, but none of that shit is our concern as of five-thirty today."

FAMILY - AN ODYSSEY

FATHER
(MONOLOGUE)

We stopped talking long enough, for the wait staff to clear the table and she went to the ladies room, I asked for two fresh water glasses, and a new bottle of *San Pellagrino* water, we had been coming here every Friday night, for so many years they all knew that when I asked for our special bottle of aged bourbon from the manager's office, that we were going to be here for a couple more hours, they simply left us alone.

FATHER

"Hey remember that bottle of old aged Bourbon, we went halves on with our first paychecks from there?"

PARALEGAL

"Yeah so your wife, and my girlfriend at the time wouldn't notice, we lied and told them that was our take home I stashed money away for four years, while I was with her."

FATHER

"I just told my wife I got a raise."

PARALEGAL

"What did you do with that money?"

FATHER

"Trust fund for him, you?"

PARALEGAL

"Condo in Malibu."

FATHER

"That's worth a pretty penny now."

PARALEGAL

"A trust fund doesn't sound like a 'shitty father' thing to do to me, actually that's a pretty great father thing to do, don't you think?"

FATHER

"Not really, no one knows about it except me, and now you."

PARALEGAL

"Hence another reason to re-connect with your son, just sayin'."

FATHER

"Anyway about the Bourbon, I kept it here in a secret place let's open it."

PARALEGAL

"Hell yeah!"

FATHER

"Remember, you don't open a special bottle of aged Bourbon unless you're with friends and or family, and you're not in a hurry to go anywhere."

FAMILY - AN ODYSSEY

PARALEGAL
"This is our last Friday night together, I'm not going anywhere."

FATHER
(MONOLOGUE)
Over the next three and a half hours, I tell my only friend and career long paralegal, everything I've done on my son's behalf in the shadows of his life, when her phone rings, I know we will be wrapping up our ritual Friday night, for the last time.

PARALEGAL
"Hey babe I'm coming home to you right now, love you bye."

FATHER
"So, what are you going to do on Monday?"

PARALEGAL
"Well wifey and I are going to travel, she wants to learn to cook authentic food in their native countries, like Brazil Greece, Italy etcetera, what are you going to do?"

FATHER
"Beyond selling the house, I haven't really thought about it."

PARALEGAL
"You and I both know what you should do, you don't have that many more trips around this sun."

FATHER
"While your wife is learning to cook all that food, what are you going to be doing besides, eating it?"

PARALEGAL
"Classic avoidance, but I'll play for a minute, I'm going to continue to write…

FATHER
"What, when did you start writing?

PARALEGAL
"That first Friday night, I went home and just wrote for about two hours I've been doing that for all the years we've worked together, every Friday night do you know how many books get written in two hours a week, every week?"

FATHER

"I have no idea."

PARALEGAL

"A lot now back to you, sell that damn house and move your ass into one of those "Active Senior Adult" whatever communities in Las Vegas, and fucking re-connect with your son before you die, do you hear me- Before. You. Fucking. Die!"

FATHER

"Okay. Okay."

PARALEGAL

"Don't fucking 'okay okay' me, promise me, no give me your word."

FATHER

"I give you my word, that I will re-connect with my son before I die."

PARALEGAL

"Thank you, now I have to get home to my hot wife, have a beautiful rest of your life my friend."

FATHER

"Thanks my friend, have a beautiful rest of your life, with your hot wife."

FATHER

(MONOLOGUE)

I watch my best friend and career long paralegal put on her coat, walk out the door and get into a waiting cab, for probably the last time, I grab my own coat and the now empty aged bottle of bourbon we bought so many years ago, I leave two hundred dollars on the table, and walk out the door for most likely the last time into my own waiting cab.

(CONTINUING)

I know a real estate agent for high end homes, here in the San Fernando Valley when I told her that I wanted to close escrow in less than thirty days, she informed me that was almost unheard of until she heard what her bonus would be on top of her commission, I'm never surprised at how large amounts of money incentivizes people to get their shit together quick, fast, and in a hurry twenty days after putting the house on the market, the realtor came by with the papers to close.

L.A. REALTOR

"Okay sign here, initial here, and sign again right here, now this house is no longer yours."

FATHER
(MONOLOGUE)

As I signed off on my life here in L.A., I really didn't feel anything, oh well c'est la vie.

SON

"Oh...My...God, what the actual fuck?"

FATHER

"Hello son, can I come in?"

SON

"No you may not come in, you may return to whichever level of *Dante's Inferno* that's reserved for lawyers, who happen to be shitty fathers."

FATHER

"I'm sure I deserve that, but son we need to talk."

SON

"Don't call me 'son', you don't get that privilege."

FATHER

"Fair enough, but that doesn't negate the fact, that we need to talk."

FATHER
(MONOLOGUE)

Suddenly the ringtone of *Somewhere Over the Rainbow* fills the air between us, even dressed casually in black jeans and a gray t-shirt with *Louboutin* loafers, he's still striking.

SON

"Hello... yeah um... I have a situation here... I don't know... you sure? Okay, thanks."

FATHER
(MONOLOGUE)

Stepping over the threshold into my son's home, I was surprised at the stark minimalism, and felt instantly ashamed at the presumptive stereotypes, I held toward him all these years.

SON

"Your ass caught a break, the office doesn't need me right now."

FATHER

"Thanks, s... thanks."

SON

"Wait a minute, how did you find me?"

FATHER

"That's something of a long story."

SON

"'*Cliff Notes*' version, I don't have all day."

FATHER

"Very well then, a former client is an acquaintance of yours, he text me your address after I landed at the airport."

SON

"Who?"

FATHER

"The who's not important."

SON

"You don't get to dictate what's important here, especially after the shit you pulled last month."

FATHER

"I didn't think you knew it was me, why didn't you say anything?"

SON

"I knew it was you, because you're the only man alive that I know, who still wears *Old Spice* cologne.

Oh and the card you left, was from the law firm you worked at my whole life except when I called that Monday, I was told you had retired so I burned it, and vowed never to purposely see your face again, yet here you stand- fuck me!"

FATHER
(MONOLOGUE)

His anger and dare I assume hurt, at my fumbled attempt to reach out to him at the lounge caught me a little off guard, I had to sit down.

FATHER

"I'm sorry about the card, it's the only thing I had, and...

SON

"So, you give me a number where you no longer work? What kind of shit is that?"

FATHER

"I know, and I was vividly reminded of that mistake, by my friend and former paralegal, believe me she was as angry as you are actually more so, she's the one who insisted that I come here to try and re-connect with you."

SON

"Re-connect with me, what the fuck for? You kicked me out of the house when I was fifteen."

FATHER

"I was shocked, I was grieving, I didn't know what to do."

FATHER
(MONOLOGUE)

We were both standing a coffee table apart, it might as well have been an ocean, an immovable object meeting an angry irresistible force.

SON

"I was grieving as well, I lost my better half, we were each other's better half I was honoring my mother, in my way by wearing her *Coco Chanel* skirt suit, I borrowed the gloves, hat and heels from my favorite aunt, who took me in."

FATHER
(MONOLOGUE)

I have hated myself a bit, for telling my own son that I would not, and could not accept him for who he was as a teenager, I need him to accept me now, as his dying father karma is a real bitch.

FATHER

"You have to understand son, it was the same suit that I had to borrow money for, so she could buy it for our wedding day at City Hall, you wearing it at her funeral was too much for me, I know that was a pretty shitty thing to say to my own son, and I'm so so sorry for that amongst, other things."

SON

"You can take your apologies, and shove them up your ass, I..."

FATHER

"You're not making this easy for me!"

SON

"What? Easy for you, did you literally think that you could show up at my door, after almost two decades of radio silence, drop a few 'I'm sorry's' and then we'd be all good?"

FATHER

"Frankly, yes."

SON

"Get the fuck out of my house, now!"

FATHER

"Son wait, please listen I know I've made some horrible mistakes, but I was trying to do what I thought a man was supposed to do right out of law school, I was trying to make partner to provide a better life for my family, that's what a man's supposed to do."

FATHER
(MONOLOGUE)

I was getting exhausted, and a little dizzy, I needed a drink bad but I was in this shit now, and I had to shovel it.

SON

"What about what a husband is supposed to do? What about what a father is supposed to do? Didn't bone up on those two chapters in the 'what a man's supposed to do' manual, did you?"

FATHER

"How the hell would you know, what a husband and father is supposed to do? You dress up in women's clothes, for godsake."

SON

"I know because, I've experienced them in the homes of my chosen family, and for your edification, I don't 'dress up in women's clothes' I get dressed!"

FATHER

"Same difference, a man's not supposed to dress like a woman unless..."

SON

"Unless what, and you had better choose your next words very carefully."

FATHER

(MONOLOGUE)

I had to sit down again and he followed suit, breathing slowly and deeply, I realized either sitting or standing, we are the same physical height, but emotionally he towers over me.

FATHER

"I didn't want this, I didn't want our first daytime meeting, in two decades to be like this, I'm sorry I'm not doing this right, I'm sorry my words are coming out all wrong, I'm out of my depth here, I'm a lawyer I'm used to convincing people of shit."

SON

"Well, my whole life you've convinced me that you're a shitty father, good job."

FATHER

"Will you give me a fucking break here, I'm trying to make amends, I'm trying to keep a promise to an old friend, that I will never see again."

SON

"Why? Are they dying?"

FATHER

"No son, I am."

SON

"Goodbye, and don't ever call me that again."

FATHER

(MONOLOGUE)

I found myself on the other side of his door, noticing the rainbow letters spelling out "WELCOME" hanging from a small hook on the door jam, walking down the steps dialing up the *Mandalay Bay* Concierge desk, I wonder how many times can I fuck this shit up with him, while karma joyously kicks my ass six ways to Sunday before I quite literally run out of time, tick fucking tock! I asked for a car to pick me up, I had no idea as to where I was oh great, I'm getting that damn chatty driver, and the hits just keep on coming.

RECEPTIONIST

"Good afternoon sir, how may I serve you?"

FATHER

"Hi, I'm looking for...

RECEPTIONIST

"Oh I know you, I've seen your picture!"

FATHER

"I assure you young lady, I have never been in this building therefore, you can't possibly know me."

RECEPTIONIST

"Wait just a minute, see here you are with our CEO at a charity gala in L.A. so yeah I do know you, your law firm's our corporate attorneys."

FATHER

"Well shit you got me, congratulations."

RECEPTIONIST

"Thanks it's my job to know all the higher ups, their family members and important -what I like to call satellite people- and you sir are a satellite person, also the father of the best date I've ever had."

FATHER

"Yeah about him, where...?

RECEPTIONIST

"Gone."

FATHER

"When will he be back?"

RECEPTIONIST

"Never."

FATHER

"Are you being paid by the word?"

RECEPTIONIST

"Sir, your son resigned his position as lead designer last month, we had quite a send-off event for him in one of the ballrooms at *MGM*.

And on a personal note, he is now the yardstick by which I measure all of the men I date, whoever he decides to marry, is going to be the luckiest person breathing air."

FAMILY - AN ODYSSEY

FATHER
"Wow really well good for you, thanks and good luck to you, goodbye."
RECEPTIONIST
"Have an excellent day, sir."

FATHER
(MONOLOGUE)
Oh my God I feel like fucking *Columbo*, but instead of piecing together clues to find out 'whodunnit' I'm trying to find out who he is, who the fuck is my son and why am I suddenly jealous of him? Thank God we can go to bars again, I need a couple of bourbon and waters ASAP.

I like that chandelier in the *Cosmopolitan* and their bourbon selection isn't half bad, probably should eat something, don't know if this headache is from hunger or frustration the good thing about dying, is that you get really specific about what you want to eat and drink, and where you'd rather not die and doing what, I know I'd rather not die trapped in a car with that chatty driver, all the way to the *Cosmopolitan* though.

SON

"Oh my fu... what are you doing here? I cannot do this right now, I'm running late, and my fucking driver isn't here yet...

FATHER

"I have a car and driver, I'll take you anywhere you want to go, we can talk."

SON

"Absolutely no... shit fine, but I don't want to hear one single solitary word from you, understand?"

FAMILY - AN ODYSSEY

FATHER

"Completely just one thing, and I promise not another word."

SON

"What?"

FATHER

"You look beautiful."

SON

"Uh, oh, thanks, that was unexpected."

FATHER

"May I?"

FATHER
(MONOLOGUE)

As I presented my arm to my son, I kept telling myself to just breathe slowly, as he looped his arm through mine, I felt his gloved fingers grip a little tighter as we descended the steps of his condo, walking carefully to my waiting car with that chatty driver, I leaned in the passenger window and told him not to say a word.

(CONTINUING)

Opening the back passenger door I helped him in, feeling the satin of his fingertips in my bare hand, in that moment I felt my stomach and heart grow very warm.

After gently closing the door, I took a few seconds to lean against the trunk, and take several deep breaths to absorb the fact that my son doesn't dress up in women's clothes, my son gets dressed.

(CONTINUING)

Inside the car, I was glad for the silence because for the first time in my life, I didn't have words that probably would have ruined this delicate truce my son, and I have finally forged.

Arriving at the lounge, where I had gently stalked him two months ago, there were enough differences to make this Saturday night not quite déjà vu but somewhat familiar, the jazz singer and her band were in the middle of an Ella Fitzgerald song, as we garnered two seats at the bar, apparently reserved for him and his stole, which he neatly folded onto his lap.

For the next two and a half hours, we sat in complete silence as we consumed two *Tanqueray* martinis with Greek olives, and smoked two of our Mexican brand cigarettes apiece.

When he was ready to leave I helped him with his stole, and escorted him to and through the door, as well as opening the car door helping him in and closing it, breathing against the trunk and then settling into the silent bubble.

(CONTINUING)

The silence was broken by him, standing at his front door eye level with the rainbow "WELCOME" letters.

SON

"Would you like to come by for lunch on Monday, say two o'clock?"

FATHER

"Yes, I'd like that, yes."

SON

"Okay, calm down."

FATHER

"Sorry."

SON

"Thanks for this evening, goodnight."

FATHER

"Goodnight so..., goodnight."

FATHER
(MONOLOGUE)

When I heard the deadbolt click home, I sank down onto the top step sighed deeply and whispered a "thank you" to my only friend, who was God knows where with her hot wife.

(CONTIUING)

I'm starting to get the lay of the land here in Las Vegas, and this chatty driver has become my "white noise" when I'm in the car.

I think that's actually his superpower to drone on and on about nonsensical shit, so that his passengers can concentrate on what they need to, I've come to think that's actually pretty cool.

While resort hotel living is great and all, after a very short while it becomes fucking monotonous and damned boring so, I've asked the Concierge desk to find a real estate agent, specializing in "Active Adult" communities, or housing for fifty-five plus people, who are basically senior citizens.

(CONTINUING)

The desk connected me with this weird woman, who wore way the hell too many noisy bangles on her left arm, she and I had driven all over town seen ten communities a couple of them twice because she has the attention span of a cat, I decided on the one that's ten minutes from my son's condo complex with the serene name *Las Vegas Meadows* established in the eighties.

This community of concrete based mobile homes, feels like a meadow in the desert the palm trees really sell it, I chose a spacious three bedroom, two bath home close to one of the two pools there seems to be shit going on all the time here, with a clubhouse with billiard and card tables, a banquet room and a goddamn piano on a stage, these seniors are living it the fuck up in here, hell yeah this is where I'm going to die!

(CONTINUING)

I invited the agent up, to have lunch in my suite at the *Mandalay Bay* room service was impeccable with a special choice of aged bourbon, which I've grown accustomed to and opened after they cleared everything away.

FATHER

"Now let's get down to brass tacks, how much is it going to cost me, and when can I move in?"

LV REALTOR

"Oh, this is good bourbon!"

FATHER

"Yeah."

LV REALTOR

"Okay see we have to run your credit background, employment history etcetera etcetera, that could take about five to seven, maybe even ten business days barring of course any snags, spaces or holes in your work history, and assuming of course that you're not a criminal."

FATHER

"How long, if I pay in cash up front?"

LV REALTOR

"Less."

FATHER

(MONOLOGUE)

As always money talks and bullshit walks, I was in my new house three days later, it nearly fucking killed me to have to postpone that lunch, for the two weeks it took me to be ten minutes closer to him.

FATHER

"Hi, I don't know if you've ever had bourbon, but I thought that we could share this one sometime."

SON

"Interesting, *Buffalo Trace* cute bottle, thanks."

FATHER

"Should I take off my shoes? I noticed you did that, the last time...

SON

"Yeah sure, thanks I'm not going to tell you, how many times I undressed, dressed and redressed for this lunch."

FATHER

"Well you look great, I appreciate your thoughtfulness, if it makes you feel any better, I think I got about thirty minutes of sleep last night."

SON

"Yeah it does, I remember the night before you had a trial, nothing short of a dynamite blast next to your head would wake you."

FATHER

"I...

SON

"Wine? I'm partial to Cabernet."

FATHER

"Great."

SON

"I made tapas and crème' brule', you cool with that?"

FATHER

"Absolutely, nice place you have here, if not a little sparse... I'm sorry, I didn't mean that to come out as any kind of criticism."

SON

"It's fine you should have seen it before, me and the girls caught the *Marie Kondo* bug."

FATHER

"The girls? Also, who or what is a '*Marie Kondo*'?"

SON

"Here, sit, cheers."

FATHER

"Cheers."

SON

"The girls are my chosen family, and *Marie Kondo* is the world famous tidying-up guru."

FATHER

"At the risk of pissing you off, people don't choose their family, they are born into whichever one they land in."

SON

"I can't get pissed off at ignorance."

FATHER

"Right, so... is there more wine?"

SON

"Sure."

FATHER

"I'm sorry, I guess I just don't understand your lifestyle."

SON

"My lifestyle?"

FATHER

"Well, the whole getting dressed thing, admittedly I don't know anything about the trans...

SON

"Whoa, what?"

FATHER

"*Jenner* and *Cher*'s kid...

SON

"Oh. My. God. no, no, no!"

FATHER

"Then what the hell, son?"

SON

"Okay let's just take a breath, I'm going to check on lunch."

FATHER
(MONOLOGUE)

Fuck, fuck, fuck! Is there any other way, I can possibly shit this bed any worse? I highly fucking doubt it, the only way I can drive him further away from me, is in a car.

SON

"Here, let's just not talk for a while, okay?"

FATHER

"Okay, I'm sorry, I...

SON

"Shh... no words right now."

FATHER
(MONOLOGUE)

This silence was deafening, pulsating louder and harder with decades of tension, this ticking time bomb that is this relationship could blow us apart, for the rest of my short life well, literally saved by the bell.

SON

"Do you want to set the table?"

FATHER

"Yes."

SON

"Plates are in that cabinet, silverware in the drawer by the sink, napkins on the other side of the fridge in the tray."

FATHER

"Got it."

FATHER
(MONOLOGUE)

I must admit, he has excellent taste in dinnerware, he seems to be partial to square and cubed shapes, not unlike his mother's eye toward the exquisite and expensive, and she always wondered why I was rarely home for family dinners.

SON

"I'm going to explain something to you, and I would really rather not hear your voice until I'm done, cool?"

FATHER

"Cool."

SON

"Granted, we don't get to choose the family we are born into, but a family or group of people who have knitted themselves into a family, can choose you and when they do it is much like adoption.

And you get a day that is celebrated, called a 'Gotcha' day sort of a second Birthday the girls and I are a knitted together family, and earlier this week we celebrated our fifteenth 'Gotcha' day.

(CONTINUING)

I am neither a transexual, transvestite, nor am I transgender, those are all different personalities and pronouns, I'm sexually attracted to women but I do feel more comfortable in vintage designer women's clothing.

When I wear men's clothes, it feels like I'm armoring up to do battle, and that's exhausting which is one of the reasons I left the company after a decade.

I've always dreamed of creating something of my own, in the heart of the *Arts District* so, I hope I've set you straight about my 'lifestyle' do you want dessert?"

FATHER

"Wow, I'm going to need a couple of minutes to wrap my head around all this, so yeah, I could use some dessert."

SON

"Okay, um, I've never had bourbon you want to open this?"

FATHER

"Sure, what kind of water do you have? It's better that way, opens it up and smooths out the rough edges."

SON

"I've got *San Pellegrino* in the fridge, and while you're over there, grab a couple of those smaller glasses."

FAMILY - AN ODYSSEY

FATHER
(MONOLOGUE)

I can feel my body winding down, tired and getting winded a little too often, but I can't let this fuck up the goodwill my son has been extending toward me for Thanksgiving.

I'm finally going to meet his "family" I can't lie, I'm a bit apprehensive I did get through the Saturday night at the lounge, when he was dressed twice, I don't have the time not to be okay with having my last Thanksgiving with three drag queens, and my son who likes to get dressed.

FATHER

"Well son I see what you mean about family, everyone should have at least one person on this planet, who gives a shit about their ass, and you've got three."

SON

"You told me you had a friend, that you promised to come here for."

FATHER

"Not anymore, she's writing and eating her way around the world, we said our goodbye's in L.A."

SON

"Yeah, about this 'I'm dying' that's not a real thing, is it?"

FATHER

"Hey grab some glasses, and I'll tell you about the documentary that got me turned onto this *Buffalo Trace* bourbon."

SON

"You... watched... a documentary."

FATHER

"Since I bought my laptop, and discovered these streaming services, who needs television?

Where's this *Hulu* and *Netflix* been all my life?"

SON

"Having not been created yet."

FATHER
"Come on smart-ass, let me tell you a thing or two about bourbon."

FATHER
(MONOLOGUE)

We spent hours talking, I didn't expect him to make up his sofa bed and ask me to stay, we haven't slept under the same roof since he was a teenager I came here to re-connect with him, and I think I have to the only extent I can.

I know it's too little and way the fuck too late, but I hope in the end he can if not understand at least accept, that all I could ever do was not what I wanted, which was to be a writer but what I had to do, which was to be an attorney.

SON
(MONOLOGUE)

I guess his 'I'm dying' really was a thing, it's weird so soon after Thanksgiving and so close to Christmas, just drops dead in the middle of a *Ninety-nine Cent Store* parking lot, buying Christmas decorations, not that far from his brand new car.

I don't feel as bad as I felt, when my favorite aunt and uncle died in a traffic accident, more like an acquaintance you're becoming better friends with, a little sad but not that broken up about it.

(CONTINUING)

The hospital personnel bagged his personal effects, called both numbers in his phone- my seven oh two and his friend's two one three, interrupting me and the girls consuming champagne and canapes.

Having just signed the lease on our three-story building, that'll house our vintage designer consignment space, *Undressed Dressed Redressed*.

Thanksgiving night was pretty good, I guess that's what these holidays are supposed to be all about, forgiveness understanding and the girls reminded me about acceptance, that he did the best he could with what he had, and who he was at that time.

Well, he wanted to leave me something to remember him by *Buffalo Trace* bourbon and all this money, mission accomplished thanks Dad, cheers.

SON

"Hi how are you? Welcome, how was your flight?"

PARALEGAL

"First class is always great."

SON

"Yeah it is make yourself comfortable, you can leave your shoes on the runner by the door, if you don't mind."

PARALEGAL

"All cool, I've grown accustomed to bein' bare foot these last few months."

SON

"Well I have Cabernet, Bourbon and..."

PARALEGAL

"You had me at Bourbon."

SON

"*San Pellegrino* water okay?"

PARALEGAL

"Absolutely, that was our favorite combo back in L.A."

SON

"Please sit, cheers."

PARALEGAL

"Cheers I like how much open space you have here, feels like you can breathe, were you bitten by the *Marie Kondo* bug?"

SON

"Guilty as charged, I made empanadas with spinach and kale salad, and crème' brule' for lunch, hope you're hungry."

PARALEGAL

"What are you, a baby *Gordon Ramsey*?"

SON

"Oh I wish, I just love the *Food Network*, really just any cooking show."

PARALEGAL

"I never pegged the desert for such gorgeous weather, only either fryin' or freezin'."

SON

"Everything in Vegas is a roll of the dice, the weather's no different.

PARALEGAL

"That's funny!"

SON

"I set the table on the balcony, shall we?"

PARALEGAL

"Lead the way."

PARALEGAL

"This is impressive, so good!"

SON

"Thank you, I really wanted to impress you."

PARALEGAL

"Why?"

SON

"Because you and my father had a decades long, I'm guessing not just a working relationship."

PARALEGAL

"What?"

SON

"He's dead, so you don't have to deny it now."

PARALEGAL

"Again, what?"

SON

"Okay were you and he, having an affair all those years?"

PARALEGAL

"Oh God No!"

SON

"Why do you say it like that?"

PARALEGAL

"Listen I'm gay, when your father and I met that first day at the law firm I was in a long-term relationship, his and your mother's marriage was already on the rocks."

SON

"So, you and he never..."

PARALEGAL

"Not even if I were straight, he had too much baggage."

SON

"You're not wrong there."

PARALEGAL

"Look, I'm sorry if you thought I was the source of your parent's problems but I promise you I wasn't, they were in an emotionally damaged vortex of their own makin', I was just the friend who was his life-line when he came up for air."

SON

"Well, I'm glad he had a friend like you."

PARALEGAL

"He used to tell me that I was his only friend, it's kinda sad he was a good guy, once you got to know him."

SON

"Yeah well, not everyone could get past those firewalls."

PARALEGAL

"That's so true."

SON

"Thank you for being his friend."

PARALEGAL

"It was a tough job but somebody had to do it, thank you for a lovely lunch, look over everything here at your leisure if you have any questions, comments or concerns hit me up."

SON

"Again, thank you for making the trip."

PARALEGAL

"No problem, oh before I forget come Valentine's Day, wifey and I will be ten minutes away, the son-of-a-bitch left me his house!"

SON

"Really, in that case I'd like to be friends."

PARALEGAL

"Yeah I'm cool with that, see you in a couple of months."

SON

(MONOLOGUE)

I did not expect her to be so cool.

SON

"Welcome, I'm glad you could make it."

RECEPTIONIST

"Thanks for the invite, I thought you forgot about me."

SON

"Of course not, you're unforgettable and you look amazing!"

RECEPTIONIST

"I thought you might appreciate a *Diane von Furstenberg.*"

SON

"Uh yeah, the dress as well."

RECEPTIONIST

"Oh my, thank you."

SON

"Champagne?"

RECEPTIONIST

"Yes, please."

SON

"May I?"

RECEPTIONIST

"Surely, someone has snatched you off the market."

SON

"No I'm afraid I'm still wandering the aisles, honestly I haven't been looking, I've had a lot on my plate."

RECEPTIONIST

"Oh yeah, I heard about your Father, I'm sorry."

SON

"Thanks but I didn't really mean that, I meant this place bringing it to life, after so many years of planning and dreaming, quitting the office is when the real work began."

RECEPTIONIST

"Please, tell me more."

SON

"Really?"

RECEPTIONIST

"Absolutely you are the most interesting, thoughtful, kind and simply gorgeous man, I've ever had the pleasure of one date with."

SON

"I'm sorry I never called you, truth is I lost your number, and I was too embarrassed to ask you for it again."

RECEPTIONIST

"Oh My God all this time, I thought I wasn't impressive enough for you, after all I'm just a damn good receptionist."

SON

"Not impressive enough? Receptionist by day, *Shakespearean* actress by night!"

RECEPTIONIST

"You know about my acting? How?"

SON

"One of the girls is in your acting troupe."

RECEPTIONIST

"Who?"

SON

"The who's not important, what is important is that I bought the DVD of *Much Ado About Nothing,* and watched it before I went to *Bard in the Bar* at the *Velveteen Rabbit,* and again at the *Lovelady Brewing Company,* so that I knew what was going on when you guys where performing and might I add, that was the most inventive way I have ever seen that play performed.

Also you were the loveliest fairy queen I'd ever seen, when you guys performed *A Midsummer's Night Dream* in Sunset Park for *Shakespeare in the Park,* and I watched the *YouTube* performance of *Julius Caesar/ Cleopatra,* indeed the show must go on even during a pandemic."

RECEPTIONIST

"Oh my, so you've been gently stalking me?"

SON

"No more like being the superfan, you never knew you had."

RECEPTIONIST

"I could kiss you right now."

SON

"What's stopping you?"

RECEPTIONIST

"This champagne glass."

SON

"May I?"

RECEPTIONIST

"Yes, please."

SON

MONOLOGUE)

It's not the first time, I've unwrapped a woman wearing a *DVF* wrap-dress, but I do intend to make it the last time.

RECEPTIONIST

"This *Valentine's Day*, is absolutely the best one I've ever had."

SON

"The day's not over yet for you my love, I have a surprise in *Dressed* I hope you like it"

RECEPTIONIST

"I like everything in that showroom!"

SON

"Well, you say that..."

RECEPTIONIST

"Dammit, just show me already!"

SON

"Okay okay close your eyes, and give me your hand."

SON
(MONOLOGUE)

I've thought about how I wanted to propose to her, since the morning after the grand opening, I wanted something so jaw-dropping and so memorable, she'd re-tell it every chance she got for the rest of her life.

When it came in it was my day down in *Undressed*, where all the garments are evaluated, sorted and cleaned, I took personal charge of it every step of the way.

Up in *Redressed* I took every pain and care to repair its tiny flaws, it was lighter than and more delicate than air.

This was going to be my proposal present, to the woman who would finally take me off the market down on bended knee, in our fabulous center-stage showroom *Dressed*.

SON

"Okay my love, open your eyes."

RECEPTIONIST

"Oh My God is this a... is this THE... *Vera Wang*? Is this really happening?"

SON
(MONOLOGUE)

I knelt down in front of her, standing in front of her very own *Vera Wang* wedding gown, shortened to just above her knee I pulled *The Leo* princess cut diamond engagement ring out of my back pocket, and asked her...

FAMILY - AN ODYSSEY

SON

"May I?"

SON
(MONOLOGUE)

She extended her shaking, tastefully manicured left hand, and whispered...

RECEPTIONIST

"Yes, please!"

FAMILY- AN ODYSSEY VALERIE J RUNYAN
FAMILY- AN ODYSSEY VALERIE J RUNYAN
FAMILY- AN ODYSSEY VALERIE J RUNYAN
FAMILY- AN ODYSSEY VALERIE J RUNYAN
FAMILY- AN ODYSSEY VALERIE J RUNYAN
FAMILY- AN ODYSSEY VALERIE J RUNYAN
FAMILY- AN ODYSSEY VALERIE J RUNYAN
FAMILY- AN ODYSSEY VALERIE J RUNYAN
FAMILY- AN ODYSSEY VALERIE J RUNYAN
FAMILY- AN ODYSSEY VALERIE J RUNYAN
FAMILY- AN ODYSSEY VALERIE J RUNYAN
FAMILY- AN ODYSSEY VALERIE J RUNYAN
FAMILY- AN ODYSSEY VALERIE J RUNYAN
FAMILY-AN ODYSSEY VALERIE J RUNYAN
FAMILY- AN ODYSSEY VALERIE J RUNYAN
FAMILY- AN ODYSSEY VALERIE J RUNYAN
FAMILY- AN ODYSSEY VALERIE J RUNYAN
FAMILY- AN ODYSSEY VALERIE J RUNYAN
FAMILY- AN ODYSSEY VALERIE J RUNYAN
FAMILY- AN ODYSSEY VALERIE J RUNYAN
FAMILY- AN ODYSSEY VALERIE J RUNYAN
FAMILY- AN ODYSSEY VALERIE J RUNYAN
FAMILY- AN ODYSSEY VALERIE J RUNYAN

CHAPTER IV. PAGEANT

SON

Ladies, mail call!

QUEEN 1

Ooh goody goody, I hope I get something good!

QUEEN 2

You always get something...

QUEEN 1

Yeah, but it's not always good.

QUEEN 3

Well at least you get something, I'm "persona non grata" over here.

QUEEN 2

Now where did I leave my tiny violin?

QUEEN 3

Oh fuck you!

QUEEN 2

Maybe later for lunch darling, I already had breakfast.

SON

Hey, remember no claws before noon.

Now let's see who gets what here.

Vogue for you...

QUEEN 1

Yay!

QUEEN 3

I can't believe you still get that.

QUEEN 1
Style never expires!

SON
Food Network Magazine and *Food and Wine,* for our resident chef...

QUEEN 2
Yes Yes Yes!

QUEEN 3
The only reason I don't eat out anymore.

QUEEN 1
Sure that's the ONLY reason?

QUEEN 3
Bitch, I will...

SON
Hey, what is it with you two?
Calm the fuck down, last time!
My *Entrepreneur Magazine* and *Magnolia Journal,* oh here's something for you Ms "persona non grata"

QUEEN 3
Great, finally!

QUEEN 1
Finally, what?

QUEEN 2
Yeah, great what?

SON
Care to share with the rest of the class?

QUEEN 3
Okay fine, I didn't want to say anything 'cause I didn't want to

jinx it, that's why I've been...

QUEEN 2

Bitchy!

QUEEN 1

Impossible!

SON

Dare I say, cranky!

QUEEN 3

Alright ALL OF THE ABOVE, but for good reason.

QUEEN 2

C'mon out with it, while we're still relatively young.

QUEEN 3

Well, most of us...

SON

ANYWAY!

QUEEN 3

Yeah right, a while ago I entered our business and my brand-new cosmetic line *Mica Shine,* as sponsors of the inaugural *Drag And Trans Pageant.*

QUEEN 1

Oh My God, no you didn't!

QUEEN 2

Without asking us?

SON

What the actual fuck?

Why would you do that?

QUEEN 3

Yes I did, yes without asking any of you, and because it's for a very worthy cause, plus being sponsors puts *D R U Consignment Boutique* higher up on the totem pole with the Chamber of Commerce, and...

SON

Stop right there, this business in case you've forgotten is a Democracy, we vote on shit that affects ALL OF US and this sure as shit affects us all!

QUEEN 3

I know that, and I'm sorry for the secrecy, and silence but you threw the invitation away...

SON

Yeah, after we all voted not to do it!

QUEEN 3

But I voted to do it!

SON

You were the dissent, majority rules.

QUEEN 3

But this could be so good for us, on so many levels...

BOSS

Be that as it may...

QUEEN 3

Please just read the letter.

QUEEN 2

Yeah, for those of us the cheap seats.

QUEEN 1

Or hard of hearing.

QUEEN 2

Bitch, you can hear somebody else's mama call you for dinner!

SON

Alright calm the fuck down, and listen will you!

Dear D R U Vintage Consignment Boutique & Mica Shine Cosmetics, thank you for your joint sponsorship of the Inaugural **IN THE SPECTRUM TRANS AND DRAG PAGEANT.**

Holy shit, what?

QUEEN 1

What 'holy shit'?

SON

*Each sponsor or combination of sponsors, must enter a representative for the pageant meaning a **Transgender** presenting or **Drag Queen** presenting contestant.*

QUEEN 2

Yay, Oh My God yes!

SON

But wait, there's more...

Each contestant must demonstrate poise, elegance, and refinement while wearing full evening gown regalia, through three rounds of scoring by a panel of judges selected from a roster of local business persons, in good standing with the Chamber of Commerce.

SON

And that's not all, folks...

*The talent portion of the scoring, will require each contestant to **SING NOT LIP-SYNCH,** any Frank Sinatra song chosen from his entire recorded catalogue.*

Once again, thank you for your support, and good luck to all.

SON

We're gonna fucking need it.

QUEEN 3

No we're not, because you've got this shit on lock honey!

SON

Don't you "honey" me, you're still on my shit list for going behind our backs with this!

QUEEN 3

But you can sing your ass off, I've heard you up there in *DRESSED,* when you thought no one else was around.

QUEEN 1

And NO ONE is more fire, than when you get dressed to go to that lounge twice a month, to get your fancy martini and exotic cigarette smokin' on!

SON

Fuck fine, at least we have some time to get this shit together.

QUEEN 3

Define "some time"...

SON

Next month?

QUEEN 3

Try next week.

SON

Are you shitting me?

QUEEN 2

Easy peasy, lemon squeezie!

QUEEN 1

You ALREADY do what's required in your sleep, plus...

SON

Except I will be fully awake, and people will be WATCHING! Maybe if we had more time, I would feel better about all this.

QUEEN 3

We only have one week instead of three, because you threw the invitation away- so that's on you!

SON

I swear you people have gone completely, utterly, and totally INSANE!

<u>QUEEN 1</u>

Where the fuck is the guy, who a couple of years ago told his own father exactly where to go and how to get there, because he bitched about how you choose to live your life?

<u>QUEEN 2</u>

Must have flown the coup, 'cause he's not in this room.

QUEEN 3

This is important, this event is bigger than your comfort zone, this is about raising awareness and providing connection, this is for people who don't have someone like you in their lives, if we don't stand up and represent NO ONE else will- I promise you that!

SON

I'm so sorry, I really didn't realize what this meant to you, I also didn't realize that there may be some kind of speech involved...

QUEEN 1

I gotcha boo, I can throw a few words together.

SON

Of course, our very own Virginia Woolf can.

QUEEN 1

Glad I wasn't one of her friends, back in her day.

QUEEN 2

Girl please, they didn't know she ripped them to shreds in her diary until after she died, otherwise they would have killed themselves!

QUEEN 3

Truth!

SON

SERIOUSLY ladies!

You three are the professionals here, you're the ones on a stage every night...

QUEEN 3

And twice on Sundays!

SON

My point is I'm just the face of this boutique, and when I get dressed and go to the lounge, that's for my own private pleasure.

QUEEN 3

Speaking of your face, I sent the video we shot over to the people at *RuPaul's Drag Race* on the Strip, as an audition for a makeup artist assistant position, I hope you don't mind.

SON

My my my you're just full of surprises today, did you happen to sign my wife and soon to be first born, over to a rich but infertile couple in California?

QUEEN 3

Well it was on my "To Do" list today, by the way how are they?

SON

They're fine thanks.

Don't change the subject, the point is...

QUEEN 2

The point is, you've taught us how to be respectable upstanding citizens in the business community, so...

QUEEN 1

We'll teach you how to be a fabulous drag queen, for the *In The Spectrum* pageant!

QUEEN 1

Where is this bitch?

QUEEN 2

I don't know, maybe...

QUEEN 1

I know one thing, in the morning all her shoes are gonna be missing their heels!

QUEEN 2

Oh that's mean, warranted but mean!

QUEEN 3

What'd I miss?

QUEEN 2

Most of it, where've you been?

QUEEN 1

You better not have been clockin' that Greek god, over by the canape's!

QUEEN 3

Who?

What?

No!

I was getting hired, to be one of the assistants to the lead makeup artist, for *RuPaul's* new stage production on the Strip and...

QUEEN 2

Oh My God, congrats girl!

QUEEN 3

Thanks, and I get to use my new makeup line *Mica Shine*, one of the queen's was my first sale, and she raved about it to everyone else including...

QUEEN 2

Did you meet *RuPaul?*

QUEEN 3

I would not be standing HERE, if I had!

QUEEN 1

Shush, they're about to announce the winner.

SON

Wow this is so surreal, thank you!

I'm so glad this sash doesn't clash with my gown, and as far as I'm concerned everyone on this stage is a winner!

As the Scarecrow in *The Wiz* said, while pulling a scrap of paper out of his head, "Heavy lays the head, of the one who wears the crown."

As the chosen representative for the *IN THE SPECTRUM* community, I am committed to being the brightest example of service, to be the lighthouse of transparency, authenticity and accountability, to be the beacon for those who identify as- queer, fluid, transgender and nonbinary, along with allies who do business in our community.

QUEEN 1

Oh My God, I'm gonna cry!

QUEEN 2

He's so beautiful, I can't believe...

QUEEN 3

He's ours, from the day we met!

QUEEN 1, QUEEN 2

Yeah, from the day we met!

SON

Right now I'd like to bring my family to the stage, my lovely wife and our soon to be plus one, and the three queens of my life who saved my life to make this night possible, everyone in this room should be so fortunate!

FAMILY- AN ODYSSEY VALERIE J RUNYAN

FAMILY- AN ODYSSEY VALERIE J RUNYAN

FAMILY- AN ODYSSEY VALERIE J RUNYAN

FAMILY- AN ODYSSEY VALERIE J RUNYAN

FAMILY- AN ODYSSEY VALERIE J RUNYAN

FAMILY- AN ODYSSEY VALERIE J RUNYAN

FAMILY- AN ODYSSEY VALERIE J RUNYAN

FAMILY- AN ODYSSEY VALERIE J RUNYAN

FAMILY- AN ODYSSEY VALERIE J RUNYAN

FAMILY- AN ODYSSEY VALERIE J RUNYAN

FAMILY- AN ODYSSEY VALERIE J RUNYAN

FAMILY- AN ODYSSEY VALERIE J RUNYAN

FAMILY-AN ODYSSEY VALERIE J RUNYAN

FAMILY- AN ODYSSEY VALERIE J RUNYAN

FAMILY- AN ODYSSEY VALERIE J RUNYAN

FAMILY- AN ODYSSEY VALERIE J RUNYAN

FAMILY- AN ODYSSEY VALERIE J RUNYAN

FAMILY- AN ODYSSEY VALERIE J RUNYAN

FAMILY- AN ODYSSEY VALERIE J RUNYAN

FAMILY- AN ODYSSEY VALERIE J RUNYAN

FAMILY- AN ODYSSEY VALERIE J RUNYAN

FAMILY- AN ODYSSEY VALERIE J RUNYAN
FAMILY- AN ODYSSEY VALERIE J RUNYAN
FAMILY-AN ODYSSEY VALERIE J RUNYAN

CHAPTER V. FAMILY

I never thought this day would come- I mean I hoped for it, dreamed about it, but was afraid to believe in it, yet here it is- my last Saturday therapy session.

While it's no *Seven Years In Tibet*, it has been an odyssey a journey none the less, through harsh terrain and brutal desert with the most unorthodox licensed psychotherapist who *Escaped From New York*, who's ring-tone is *Viva Las Vegas*!

First of all, I never thought I'd ever trust a sis-gender white male but my soon to be ex-therapist looks like "The Dude" in *The Big Loebowski,* his house could double as a less expensive studio shoot of *Graceland*, and he mic-drops his age at any and every opportunity that he sometimes creates.

I'm sure as hell gonna miss him and his cinematic references for just about everything, I literally wondered moments after stepping into his home office "What the fuck did I get myself into?" when he shouted at me from behind his huge Elvis-memorabilia laden desk, "You want the truth, you can't handle the truth!" then he told me to sit anywhere I wanted.

I chose the far corner of his blue suede sofa that could have sat ten people comfortably, then that huge ass gentle giant knelt down in front of me and softly said, "Nobody puts Baby in a corner" in the span of what felt like seconds we went from *A Few Good Men* to *Dirty Dancing* he extended his enormous right hand that had a ring on every finger, then he sat down next to me wrapped his long tattooed arm around my shoulder pulling me against him, and said matter of factly "Much work to do, we have."

As I left that unassuming ranch-style house with the circular

68

gravel driveway, I felt a few cracks in the concrete dam I'd built, I remember actually laughing out loud for the first time in forever "Holy shit, I've got my very own Yoda!"

Over the next seven years, via movie references and dialogue lines his cinematic knowledge was encyclopedic he helped me chip away at the dam, we had a real give and take relationship more like best friends than therapist and patient.

We had some things in common- both born and raised in big cities, both our mothers committed suicide, both our fathers were for the most part absent from our lives during our formative years, movies were his solace drawing was mine I got my two degrees from UNLV and College of Southern Nevada, he got both of his in California- Stanford and UCLA after the Marine Corp.

The first time I encountered, his extremely large gun-metal gray Bull Mastiff "Sarg" he scared the shit out of me he told me what "Semper Fi" meant and one of the tattoos on his massive right forearm says "SHOCK AND AWE" I asked him why psychiatry he replied, bones aren't the only things on the human body that needs mending and besides he gets to wear his rings and display his tats!

We chipped away at why I like to "get dressed" and why I feel more comfortable not wearing all that corporate armor, even though I wore it for a decade golden handcuffed with the title of "Lead Designer" with the salary of "Founding Partner" not doing what I wanted to do- which was anything and everything having to do with vintage fashion, but what I had to do- which was to help scale an architecture firm to seven-figures before I graciously existed, can you say "like father, like son?"

One of my biggest self-reveals certainly shocked and awed the fuck out of me, came when he suggested that I watch the movie "*The Matador*" he told me to watch for how the two main characters subconsciously morph a little bit like each by the end of the film.

The "dude" knows his shit, in what turned out to be the last six months of my father's life, he became okay with "the girls" and even accepted my "getting dressed" I've taken a real liking to *Buffalo Trace Kentucky Straight Bourbon Whiskey* and *San Pellegrino Sparkling Water,* instead of my old favorite generic liquor-store Vodka and convenience-store Tonic water.

He's retiring which is why this was our last session, he and his giant dog are leaving tomorrow for Costa Rica to spend their sunset years with some military buddies by the beach, and I'm going to spend the rest of my days in the "neon capital" of the world, with the original family I've chosen to create- my wife, my daughter, and my three queens.

FAMILY- AN ODYSSEY VALERIE J RUNYAN
FAMILY- AN ODYSSEY VALERIE J RUNYAN
FAMILY- AN ODYSSEY VALERIE J RUNYAN
FAMILY- AN ODYSSEY VALERIE J RUNYAN
FAMILY- AN ODYSSEY VALERIE J RUNYAN
FAMILY- AN ODYSSEY VALERIE J RUNYAN
FAMILY- AN ODYSSEY VALERIE J RUNYAN
FAMILY- AN ODYSSEY VALERIE J RUNYAN
FAMILY- AN ODYSSEY VALERIE J RUNYAN
FAMILY- AN ODYSSEY VALERIE J RUNYAN
FAMILY- AN ODYSSEY VALERIE J RUNYAN
FAMILY- AN ODYSSEY VALERIE J RUNYAN
FAMILY- AN ODYSSEY VALERIE J RUNYAN
FAMILY-AN ODYSSEY VALERIE J RUNYAN
FAMILY- AN ODYSSEY VALERIE J RUNYAN
FAMILY- AN ODYSSEY VALERIE J RUNYAN
FAMILY- AN ODYSSEY VALERIE J RUNYAN
FAMILY- AN ODYSSEY VALERIE J RUNYAN
FAMILY- AN ODYSSEY VALERIE J RUNYAN
FAMILY- AN ODYSSEY VALERIE J RUNYAN
FAMILY- AN ODYSSEY VALERIE J RUNYAN
FAMILY- AN ODYSSEY VALERIE J RUNYAN
FAMILY- AN ODYSSEY VALERIE J RUNYAN

AUTHOR BIO

Valerie J Runyan started writing in Los Angeles where she grew up, she has been living writing, and Independent Publishing in Las Vegas for the last three decades.

She is a Writing Life Coach and leads her own virtual writing retreat, along with a virtual read and critique group, also she is the author of a number of books across several genres.

She reads a lot and writes a lot, which leaves her no time for social media, but she does have an email address and a website where her books hang out.

inkdropspace424@gmail.com www.valeriejrunyan.com[1]

---

1.   http://www.valeriejrunyan.com

Don't miss out!

Visit the website below and you can sign up to receive emails whenever Valerie J Runyan publishes a new book. There's no charge and no obligation.

https://books2read.com/r/B-A-ETKI-ZNJTH

BOOKS 2 READ

Connecting independent readers to independent writers.

Also by Valerie J Runyan

Flash Fiction
Pieces of Me - A Collection of Essays
Gospel of the Wordsmith
Caterpillar
Polar Opposites Poetry
Jagged Fiction - A Collection
Roses with a Side of Thorns
Love Quandaries
Family - An Odyssey

Watch for more at www.valeriejrunyan.com.

About the Publisher

"Desert Lighthouse Publishing" guides spirited independent writers unto their own home shores.

Read more at https://valeriejrunyan.com/.